This book belongs to

A READ-ALOUD STORYBOOK

Adapted by Victoria Saxon

MOUSE ✺ WORKS

Find us at www.disneybooks.com for more Mouse Works fun!

The Ape Mother

A baby's cry drew Kala away from her ape family. The cry was coming from a strange house, high up in a tree's branches.

Inside the house, Kala found the baby. When she held
him, he stopped crying and began to laugh with her.
Suddenly, Sabor, a ferocious leopard, sprang at them.
Kala risked her own life to save the baby.

Kala brought the baby to her family.
"You cannot keep it," said Kerchak, the apes'
leader. "It's not our kind."

"Sabor killed his family," Kala explained.

Reluctantly, Kerchak agreed to let her raise
the child. Kala named the baby Tarzan.

As he grew, Tarzan tried to fit in with his ape family.
"I'd love to hang out with you," his friend Terk told
Tarzan. "But the guys, they need a little convincing."

"What do I gotta do?" asked Tarzan gamely.

"Well you gotta . . . uh . . . go get an elephant hair,"
Terk said.

To Terk's surprise, Tarzan leaped from the cliff and swam toward the huge creatures!

When Tarzan grabbed an elephant's tail, all the elephants began to trumpet and scramble about in fear. They started to stampede!

The charging elephants rushed through the apes' feeding area. Kerchak leaped to rescue a baby ape just in time.

At the water's edge, Terk ran to Tarzan. "Come on, buddy!" she cried. "Don't die on me." As Tantor, a baby elephant, looked on worriedly, Tarzan revived.

Then Kerchak arrived. Tarzan took all the blame for the stampede.

"Tarzan will never fit into this family," Kerchak shouted at Kala.

That evening, Tarzan knelt at the edge of a pool and looked at his reflection. Kala approached.

"Why am I so different?" Tarzan asked, placing his hands against Kala's.

Kala gently put her son's head to her heart. "Inside we're the same," she said. "Kerchak just can't see that."

Tarzan smiled. "I'll make him see it," he said. "I'll be the best ape ever!"

As Tarzan grew, he learned to swim like the hippos, swing from vines like the monkeys, and surf along mossy tree limbs.

And when Sabor attacked the apes, Tarzan swung to the rescue with his spear and saved Kerchak's life! Tarzan lifted the slain leopard and let out a victory yell.

Respectfully, Tarzan laid the slain leopard at Kerchak's feet.

Then, a gunshot rang out! Kerchak hurried the apes deeper into the jungle, but Tarzan was curious. He searched for the creature that had made the strange noise.

Strangers in the Jungle

From a treetop, Tarzan studied the first humans he had ever seen.

"Mr. Clayton, your gunshots may be scaring off the gorillas," said Jane to her guide.

"Look! A gorilla nest!" exclaimed Professor Porter, Jane's father. Porter and Clayton pressed on, looking for more nests.

As Jane sketched a baby baboon, the small creature grabbed the picture from her. Jane snatched it back and a group of angry baboons began to chase her.

She turned and ran from the mob when . . . whoosh! Tarzan swooped her into the air.

Safe at last, Tarzan looked at Jane intently. Then he placed his hand against hers. She was like him!

Tarzan pointed to himself. "Tarzan," he said.

"Jane," she replied, pointing to herself.

"Jane," Tarzan repeated, smiling.

Meanwhile, Terk, Tantor, and their friends had found the humans' camp. Terk touched the typewriter. Another ape dropped a plate. The new sounds were fun!

"I feel something happenin' here!" cried Terk. She was rollicking to an all-out jam session when Tarzan and Jane arrived.

When Tarzan led Jane into the camp, she was surprised to see how he greeted Terk. "He's one of them!" Jane gasped. Then an angry Kerchak arrived and Tarzan had to leave with his gorilla family.

Kerchak ordered the gorillas to stay away from the strangers.

Tarzan objected, "They mean us no harm!" Then Tarzan turned to his mother. "Why didn't you tell me there were others like me?" he asked. But Kala did not answer him.

The next day, Tarzan returned to the humans' camp.

Tarzan fascinated Professor Porter. "He moves like an ape but looks like a man!" Porter exclaimed.

Jane and her father taught Tarzan about the human world. Tarzan, who could imitate almost any animal in the jungle, was now quickly learning English.

Tarzan showed Jane his world, too.

One day when Tarzan arrived at the camp, he realized that Jane was leaving. The boat had arrived to take her back to England.

Clayton told Tarzan, "If only she could have spent time with the gorillas . . ."

"Then Jane would stay?" Tarzan asked. Clayton nodded, smiling slyly. "I'll do it," said Tarzan.

So Terk and Tantor distracted Kerchak while Tarzan led Jane and the others to meet his ape family.

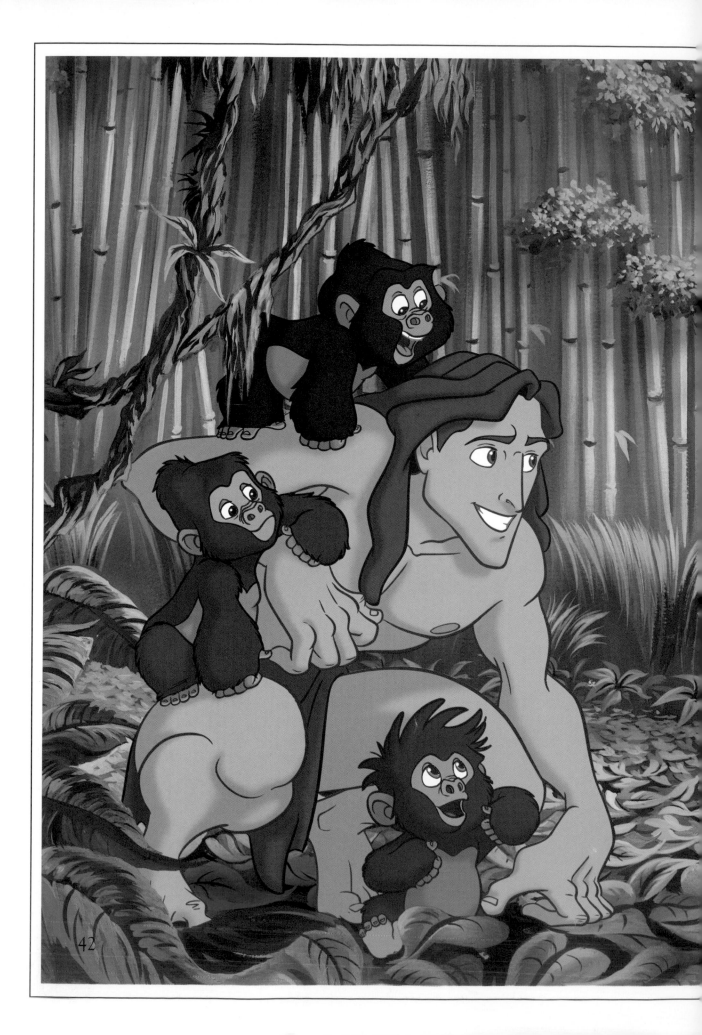

Two Worlds Meet

Jane and Porter loved the apes at first sight.

Tarzan spoke to the apes. "Oo-oo-ee-eh-ou."

Jane repeated his sounds and the baby apes cheered. "What did I say?" she asked.

"That Jane stays with Tarzan," he replied with a grin.

Then Kerchak returned—just as Clayton began
arguing with a gorilla. Enraged, Kerchak leaped to protect
the gorilla from Clayton.

"Run!" Tarzan shouted. He tackled Kerchak while
the humans escaped.

"You betrayed us all!" Kerchak told Tarzan.

Kala saw that Tarzan was torn between his love for his ape family and his need to be with the humans. Though she risked losing him forever, she led him to the tree house where she had found him.

Tarzan dressed in his father's clothes. Embracing Kala, he said, "No matter where I go, you will always be my mother."

Tarzan ran to the beach to catch up with Jane. Boarding the ship, Tarzan cast a sad glance back at his jungle home.

"Tarzan!" Jane cried in warning. But it was too late. Clayton and his evil companions ambushed Tarzan.

Clayton revealed his terrible plan. He wanted to capture the gorillas and sell them! Tarzan yelled in anguish—he had betrayed his family.

Tarzan's cry echoed deep in the jungle. Hearing it, Tantor charged to the rescue with Terk in tow!

With a crash, Tantor broke through the ship's deck, freeing Tarzan and the others. Tarzan swung quickly to the ape's nesting area, but Clayton had already captured Kerchak.

As Tarzan freed him, Kerchak said, "You came back."

"No, I came home," Tarzan replied.

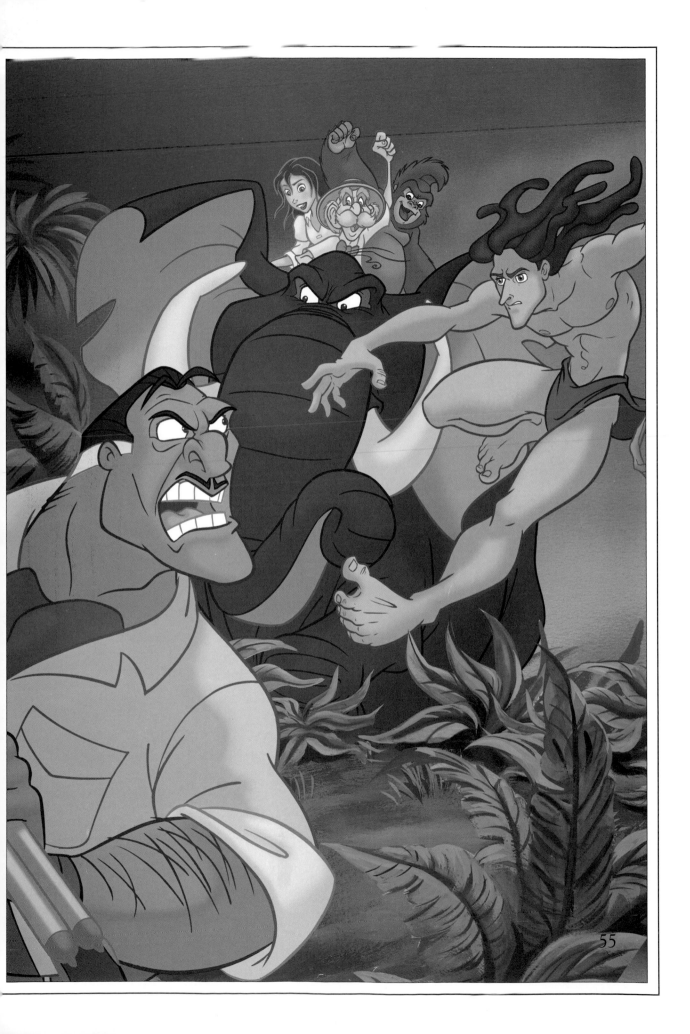

Jane and Porter arrived with Terk and Tantor. Jane swung down on a vine and knocked one of Clayton's thugs aside.

"I'm going to have you out of this in a second," she told Kala.

As Jane freed Kala, a shot rang out. Clayton had shot Tarzan in the arm! Clayton fired again, but this time Kerchak leaped between Tarzan and the bullet.

Wounded, the large ape fell to the ground. Now it was up to Tarzan to protect his family. Tarzan led Clayton up into the tall jungle trees.

Lunging at Tarzan, Clayton fell to his death.
Tarzan ran back to Kerchak. "Forgive me," Tarzan said.
With his final words, Kerchak told Tarzan, "Take
care of our family, my son."

The next day Tarzan and Jane said good-bye.

Rowing toward the ship, Porter said, "Jane, dear, I can't help feeling that you should stay. You love him."

Jane knew her father was right. She jumped out of the boat—and so did Porter!

"Oo-oo-ee-eh-ou," Jane said. She and her father were staying.

They were welcomed to their new home by all the apes . . . and by Tarzan, who knew at last where he belonged.